Flying High

Twink

Bimi

Pix

Sooze

Sili

Zena

Mariella

Lola

Book One

Flying High

Titania Woods

Illustrated by Smiljana Coh

BLOOMSBURY

LONDON BERLIN NEW YORK

Bloomsbury Publishing, London, Berlin and New York

First published in Great Britain in 2008 by Bloomsbury Publishing Plc
36 Soho Square, London, W1D 3QY

This paperback edition first published in 2009

A CIP catalogue record of this book is available from the British Library

ISBN 978 1 4088 0486 5

The paper this book is printed on is certified independently in accordance
with the rules of the FSC. It is ancient-forest friendly.
The printer holds chain of custody.

FSC

Mixed Sources
Product group from well-managed
forests and other controlled sources

Cert no. SGS - COC - 2061
www.fsc.org
© 1996 Forest Stewardship Council

Typeset by Dorchester Typesetting Group Ltd
Printed in Great Britain by Clays Ltd, St Ives Plc

1 3 5 7 9 10 8 6 4 2

www.glitterwingsacademy.co.uk

For my agent, Caroline Sheldon.
Without her wonderful support and enthusiasm,
there would be no fairies at Glitterwings.

Chapter One

'Hurry, Brownie!' whispered Twink in the mouse's ear. 'We're almost there!' Obediently, the mouse broke into a run, his whiskers shaking with every step. Twink clung to the reins. Her heart thumped as she scanned the long grass in front of them. Why couldn't she see her new school yet? They *must* be almost there by now.

And then all at once, there it was! A massive oak tree, rising up from a field of flowers. Fluttering her wings excitedly, Twink tugged at Brownie's reins.

'Look!' she shouted to her parents. 'There it is!

Glitterwings Academy!'

Twink's father swooped over her head, his purple wings beating so fast that they were a blur. 'I wondered when you'd see it!' he teased. Hovering beside her, Twink's mother squeezed her hand.

'You're going to love it here,' she said. Her bright pink hair, so much like Twink's, blew gently in the wind.

'Come on, let's hurry!' cried Twink. She nudged Brownie into a scamper and sped towards the oak tree, her parents flying close behind.

A faint buzzing noise came from the air above them. A crowd of young fairies flew into view, brightly coloured as butterflies. They dipped and swirled in the air, calling to each other.

'Good old Glitterwings!' said one. 'Isn't it great to be back?'

Twink smiled as she watched them skim off. Soon she'd be flitting about through the air with friends, too. Oh, she could hardly wait to learn to fly!

As Twink and her parents drew nearer, Glitterwings grew taller and taller, stretching up to the sky. 'It's huge!' breathed Twink. She could see hundreds of tiny windows spiralling up the tree's trunk, and a set of double doors sitting at its base.

More and more young fairies appeared, flickering about the tree like Christmas lights. They hovered together in cheerful clusters, laughing and talking. Some of them looked almost grown-up in their sparkly shorts and tank tops.

No one paid the least attention to Twink. She looked down at Brownie's round ears. Suddenly she felt very childish, riding a mouse and wearing a boring dress made of rose petals, without a sparkle in sight. Then Twink saw a lavender-haired fairy her own age on a mouse, wearing a dress made of daisies. Another First Year! She let out a relieved breath.

Hovering just above her, Twink's mother pointed out a branch. 'Look, there's Peony Branch! It's where I was when I was your age. We had so much fun there!'

'I wonder where I'll be staying?' said Twink.

The air rustled as a fairy with white wings and

sky-blue hair landed in front of them. 'I'm Mrs Lightwing, head of the First Years,' she announced, folding her wings neatly behind her back. 'And you are?' She squinted at Twink.

Twink's parents landed too, one on either side of her. They gave her encouraging smiles.

Hastily, Twink slid off Brownie and stood on her tiptoes, dipping her head politely. 'I'm Twink Flutterby,' she said.

Mrs Lightwing nodded, ticking off a name on her clover-leaf clipboard. 'Yes, you're in Daffodil Branch. Oh, and I see you went to Watercress Primary. Well, we'll expect impressive things from you in that case.' She looked sternly at Twink.

Twink gulped. 'Yes, Mrs Lightwing.' Suddenly Brownie's warm, furry nose tickled at her pocket for seeds, almost knocking her over. 'Not now, Brownie!' she hissed.

Her father laughed. 'Twink can hardly wait to learn how to fly. No more mice for her!'

Mrs Lightwing gave Twink a grudging smile. 'Just like all the other First Years. Well, I'm the Flight

mistress, so I'll be the one teaching you.'

'Oh! I mean — that's great.' Twink's heart sank. *Oh, wasps,* she thought. Flying was supposed to be fun. Mrs Lightwing looked like her face would crack if she ever *really* smiled!

Twink's father untied the oak-leaf bag that held her belongings from Brownie's back. 'Here you are, Twinkster. Your mum and I will leave now, and let you explore.'

Her mother kissed her cheek. 'Send us a butterfly every week, darling. And remember that your father and I will be at the Fairy Medics' Meeting at the end of term. We'll send someone to pick you up and bring you home for the holidays.'

'I'll remember.' Twink's eyes burned as their wings circled her warmly. Both of her parents were Fairy Medics, and Twink was hugely proud of them. She was going to miss them so much! But she wouldn't cry. Crying was as babyish as riding mice.

Then she felt guilty and gave Brownie a quick hug, wrapping her arms around his soft fur. It wasn't *his* fault that only baby fairies rode mice!

After a final squeeze, her parents flew away, waving over their shoulders. Brownie trotted along below them attached by a long cord.

'Tell Teena that I'll write to her, too,' Twink called after them. Teena, her little sister, was extremely impressed that Twink had gone to Glitterwings Academy to school. Twink smiled as she thought of Teena, and lifted her chin, determined to enjoy herself.

'Right, let's get you sorted,' said Mrs Lightwing. She steered Twink towards the ornate front door. Twink's wings rubbed together as she gazed up at

the spreading branches. What would Glitterwings be like inside?

'Here's another of our first-year fairies.' Mrs Lightwing beckoned to a fairy with long lavender hair. 'She's in Daffodil Branch, too.'

The fairy came running up, and Twink recognised the other mouse-rider she had seen earlier. The two girls smiled at each other as Mrs Lightwing introduced them. She was called Sooze, and Twink liked the look of her instantly. She had a bright, friendly face and sparkling eyes.

'I'll leave you girls here,' said Mrs Lightwing. 'Go inside and take two of the birds up to Daffodil Branch. You can choose your beds there; Mrs Hover will take care of you.' She flew off, consulting her clipboard.

Sooze laughed. 'We're opposites!' she said. And all at once Twink saw what she meant. Where Twink had pink hair and lavender wings, Sooze had lavender hair and pink wings. Both girls had pale rose-coloured skin, and violet eyes. They laughed delightedly, looking at each other.

Sooze hooked her arm through Twink's. 'We'll have to be friends, then. Opposites for ever!'

Twink's heart sang as they skipped towards the school. She had never dreamed that she'd find a friend so soon. And Sooze seemed just the sort of friend she would have wished for.

The two fairies went through the grand double doors. Twink stopped short, staring upwards. Sooze laughed. 'Haven't you seen it before, then? My sister goes here, so it's nothing new to me!'

Twink couldn't answer. She stood with her head back, drinking in Glitterwings.

The inside of the oak was smooth and hollow, and seemed filled with a golden light. Up and up it went, like the highest of towers, with brightly lit corridors shooting off in every direction, as far up as Twink could see. Those were the tree's branches, she realised. Fairies flittered everywhere, swooping and flying, darting in and out of the corridors like hummingbirds.

'It's beautiful!' Twink gasped.

Sooze nodded. 'It's great, isn't it? Come on, let's

get the birds and go and see our branch!' She tugged at Twink's hand. Near the door, a small squad of grey and yellow tits stood waiting, with jaunty red saddles perched on their backs.

Sooze hopped on the nearest one, and Twink followed, settling her bag in front of her. Her bird cocked its head, regarding her with a shiny dark eye. Twink looked doubtfully at its smooth feathers, wondering what to hold on to. She had never ridden a bird before.

'How do you –' she started.

'Daffodil Branch!' said Sooze. The two birds took

off with a rush.

'Eek!' shrieked Twink. She grabbed wildly at the glossy grey feathers, and looked down before she could stop herself – and then she wished she hadn't! The front doors were already so tiny that they looked like part of an ants' house. Oh, wasps! Her stomach lurched crazily.

'Whee!' Sooze cried. Her lavender hair blew across her laughing face. 'I can hardly wait to *really* fly,' she called across to Twink. 'But this is a lot better than riding mice!'

Twink clutched her bird's feathers as branches and classrooms sped past them. She thought she'd give anything to be back on the ground with safe, obedient Brownie!

But then as suddenly as the ride had begun, it was over. Spreading their wings, the two birds landed on a ledge with a single daffodil hanging over it. Shakily, Twink slid from her saddle as Sooze jumped off and pushed open the door.

Their branch was decorated with dozens of white and yellow daffodils. A carpet of light green moss lay underfoot. Cosy beds made of darker moss lined the curved walls, with a single large daffodil hanging upside down over each one like a canopy.

The other fairies in the room were chatting and laughing, unpacking their bags. Sooze grabbed Twink's arm. 'Come on, let's choose our beds.' The two fairies raced into the room.

There were eight mossy beds, and only two of them weren't already taken. One was at the very end of the row, and the other halfway through it. Twink stopped short in disappointment. She had hoped to have a bed beside Sooze.

Sooze just shrugged when she saw, and hopped on to the bed halfway through the row. 'I'll take this one. Lots of company!'

Twink hesitated, and looked at the fairy on the bed next to Sooze's. 'Would you like to swap?' she asked.

The fairy had silvery-green hair and lacy green wings, and wore a very posh frock made of woven dandelion petals. She stuck her pointed nose in the air.

'No, I won't swap. You should have got here

earlier, shouldn't you?'

Sooze laughed. 'Oh dear, I chose the wrong bed. Fancy having to live next to you!'

The fairy sniffed and turned away. Twink bit the inside of her cheek to keep from giggling. Going over to the last empty bed, she put her bag on it and glanced at the fairy who had the bed next to her.

Her eyes widened. She was the most beautiful young fairy Twink had ever seen, with shimmering dark blue hair and silver wings with delicate golden swirls on them. Her dress of bluebell blossoms looked so lovely on her that Twink felt plain and dull in comparison.

I'm being silly, thought Twink, tucking a strand of pink hair behind a pointed ear. *I bet she's really nice.* She smiled at the fairy.

'Hi, I'm Twink,' she said.

Colouring up, the beautiful fairy hardly even looked at her. 'I'm Bimi,' she muttered.

There was a pause. Twink slowly unpacked her things, putting the drawings of her family on top of her bedside mushroom. Finally she tried again.

'Who's that other fairy, the one in the dandelion dress?' she whispered.

Bimi shrugged. 'She's called Mariella,' she said shortly, and turned away without another word.

Twink sighed. It seemed very unfair that she had to be next to this unfriendly fairy instead of Sooze. Bimi probably thought she was too pretty to talk to someone as ordinary as Twink.

Sooze had been chatting to some of the other fairies, but now she bounced across to Twink and squeezed her hand. 'Cheer up,' she whispered. 'Even if we're not together, we're still opposites!' Twink smiled at her, feeling much better.

Suddenly a plump fairy with pale pink hair landed heavily in the doorway, puffing with exertion.

'Hello, girls!' she huffed. 'I'm Mrs Hover, the matron. Are we all settled in?' She cast an eye over the branch, and nodded with satisfaction. 'Excellent! Well, come along, everyone; there's a school assembly in two wing beats.'

Twink joined the others at the doorway. A small fleet of tits was circling just outside. Each bird in turn hopped on to the ledge to let a fairy climb on, then took off again, circling in place until every red saddle was filled.

Not again! Twink gulped. When it came to her turn, she gripped her bird's back tightly with her knees. She didn't want the other girls to see how scared she was to fly on a bird. They'd think she was a total wasp brain.

Finally Mrs Hover flew out beside them and blew a whistle. 'Right, everyone – birds to the Great Branch!'

Everywhere Twink looked, colourful lines of laughing fairies streamed through the air, heading for a large branch about midway down the tree.

'Orderly flight patterns, please!' shouted a teacher. 'Stay with your branch groups!'

Twink gripped the red saddle with clammy hands. Oh, she could hardly wait to learn how to *really* fly. She wouldn't be scared then!

The Great Branch was the largest branch of the school. Arching windows lined its curving wooden walls, with hundreds of glow-worm lanterns hanging from the ceiling like stars. Long rows of mossy tables marched down its length, with red and white spotted mushrooms for seats. A brightly coloured flower dangled upside down over each table.

'Look, there's ours!' Twink pointed to a table near the front with a cheerful yellow daffodil suspended over it. She and Sooze quickly found seats side by side, giggling as they squeezed in together, wings touching. Soon the Branch was filled with buzzing, chatting fairies.

A fairy with lavender hair and pink wings came over to their table. 'How are you getting on, Sooze?'

'Fine! Look, I've found an opposite.' Sooze pressed her head against Twink's. 'Twink, this is my sister Winn. She's a Fourth Year.'

Twink and Winn said hello to each other. Winn had the same friendly face as Sooze, with laughing purple eyes.

'Well, don't get into trouble too soon, Sooze.' Winn grinned. 'Mum told me to look after you!'

'Attention, please!' At the front of the Great Branch, a tall fairy with rainbow wings and snowy-white hair hovered above a raised platform, clapping her hands for attention.

Winn hurried back to her own table. When the room had grown so still that you could hear a bee cough, the fairy began to speak in a low, grave voice.

'To our old girls, welcome back to Glitterwings Academy. And to our new girls, a warm welcome. We hope you'll be very happy with us. I'm Miss Shimmery, the HeadFairy.'

Twink watched Miss Shimmery avidly. She seemed so calm and sure of herself, and her eyes had the faintest twinkle in them as she addressed the crowded Branch. Twink couldn't imagine that she had ever been a first-year fairy!

Miss Shimmery went on to tell the girls that from the next morning they would all be expected to wear their branch uniforms, with sashes the colour of their year. *Daffodil dresses*, thought Twink. That wasn't so bad. And the first year's colour was green, which would look pretty with yellow and white.

Across the table, Mariella sniffed. 'Daffodil dresses, how common! Mum will be furious. She wanted me to be in Orchid Branch.'

I wish you were! thought Twink.

Miss Shimmery introduced the teachers sitting at the head table. Mrs Lightwing stood up when the HeadFairy said her name, looking just as grim as before.

'First Years, your opening lesson tomorrow will be with me. We want to get you flying as soon as possible, so the bird squad can go home.'

A red-haired fairy at the Daffodil table raised her hand. She was called Pix, and Twink thought she looked very clever and serious. 'Does that mean we'll be sprinkled with fairy dust tomorrow?' she asked.

Mrs Lightwing nodded. 'Yes, you'll be sprinkled tomorrow.'

An excited murmur from the First Years filled the room. Finally, after years of waiting, they'd be sprinkled with fairy dust, giving them the magic to use their wings! Twink's heart soared. She and Sooze squeezed each other's hands, bouncing on their mushrooms. Even Mariella looked impressed.

'That's all,' said Miss Shimmery with a smile. 'Enjoy the school year.' She touched down on to the platform and waved a slim arm in the air. 'Butterflies commence!'

The softest of flapping noises filled the air as a river of jewel-coloured butterflies streamed into the room. Each carried a seed cake or a pitcher filled with fresh morning dew, which they dropped gently on to the tables.

'Thank you!' gasped Twink to the red and blue butterfly that served their table. It dipped a wing at her as it flew away.

The fairies ate hungrily, talking and laughing. When it was finally time for the First Years to mount their birds again and fly back to their branches, Twink was almost too tired to be scared.

It doesn't matter if I am, she thought as she held on to her bird. *Tomorrow I'll be sprinkled with fairy dust and I'll learn how to fly!*

Chapter Two

'Wake up, sleepyheads!' called Mrs Hover.

Twink cracked an eye open, forgetting where she was at first. All around her, fairies were sitting up in bed, yawning and smoothing their wings.

Twink sat bolt upright, her violet eyes gleaming. She was at Glitterwings Academy, in Daffodil Branch. And today she was going to learn how to fly! She bounced out of bed and ran a thistle comb through her rumpled pink hair.

'Very nice,' said Mrs Hover, coming over to her. 'Now, let's get your uniform sorted.' She had an armful of daffodils in her hands. She held one of them up against Twink. 'A nice white one for you, I think, with your pink hair. Like it?'

Twink nodded enthusiastically. 'It's beautiful.'

Mrs Hover dug into a small pouch at her hip and shook a pinch of pink and gold fairy dust on to the flower. Instantly, it formed itself into a dress Twink's size.

'Oh!' gasped Twink, and Mrs Hover laughed.

'No time to make them by hand here, with so many fairies to clothe. So we use a bit of fairy dust magic to help us along. And why not, I say? Here you go, love, put it on.'

Mrs Hover produced a woven sash of soft green grass and a jaunty cap made from an oak leaf, and a moment later Twink felt like she had been a Glitterwings girl all her life.

Sooze, similarly clothed, spun in front of her, lavender hair flying. 'Look at us!' she cried. 'Aren't we something!'

Mariella made a face as she peered into the small mirror that hung on the wall. 'Oak-leaf caps!' she

groaned. 'Don't they have any taste at all here? At home I only wore caps made of –'

'Hey, I've got a glimmery idea!' interrupted Sooze. 'Why don't you go *back* home, and stay there!'

'You shouldn't talk to Mariella like that,' squeaked a thin little fairy called Lola. She had limp blonde hair and pale blue wings. Already she and Mariella seemed to have banded together, sneering at the school and all its occupants.

'Why not?' said Sooze, taking a step forward. 'She asks for it!'

Lola paled slightly, backing up.

'Come on,' said Mariella. 'No use wasting our time on *her.*' She and Lola linked arms and turned away with a sniff, fluttering their wings grandly.

'Now, now, enough of that,' said Mrs Hover, bustling over to them. 'Don't you girls want to see your timetables? Here you go – soon you'll be kept so busy that you won't have time to squabble!'

Twink eagerly took the rose-petal timetable Mrs Hover handed her. TWINK FLUTTERBY, it said in official silver letters, with the times of all her

Mariella

classes laid out below. *Flight – Skills and Techniques. Flower Power for Beginners. Introduction to Creature Kindness. Dance for Beginners. Theory of Fairy Dust.* Twink's eyes shone. It all sounded so exciting!

She nudged Sooze with her wing. 'We've got Flower Power tomorrow! I can hardly wait – we get to heal injured flowers, and all sorts!'

'Dance, that's what *I'm* looking forward to,' said Sooze. 'All those magical moves!' She peered over Twink's shoulder and gave a little bounce. 'Look, we've got all our classes together! Glimmery!'

'All of Daffodil Branch is together,' put in Pix. 'But look, for some classes, like Flight, it's all of the first year.'

Twink's excitement faded a bit as she glanced over at Mariella and Lola. It was bad enough living with those two, without having to take every single class with them!

Never mind, at least she was with Sooze. She rolled her timetable up carefully, and put it in her rose-petal schoolbag.

Meanwhile, Mrs Hover had gone back to the dresses. She fussed over Bimi, holding up flower after flower in front of her, cooing happily. 'The yellow one? Ooh, that looks so striking with your lovely hair and wings . . . but then the white one with yellow trim would suit you so well, too . . .'

Bimi stood stiffly, her jaw set. Twink thought she looked even crosser than she had the night before. 'I don't care,' she said shortly. 'Any of them will do.'

Finally Mrs Hover chose a dress that satisfied her, and the girls gathered in the doorway to ride the birds down to breakfast. Twink bit her lip nervously

as she watched the tits circle. *Just one more time,* she told herself. *Then I'll be able to fly on my own!*

To take her mind off the birds, Twink decided to try again with Bimi. 'You look really nice,' she whispered. Mrs Hover had decided on the yellow and white dress, and it did look stunning on the blue-haired girl.

Bimi shrugged and turned away, scowling. Twink sighed. That was what she got for trying to be friendly.

Sooze let out a whoop as she climbed on her bird. 'No more birds for us after this morning!' she cried.

'Hurrah!' said a few of the other girls.

Twink climbed gingerly into a red saddle, trying to smile like the others. *Yes, and I can hardly wait!* she thought.

After breakfast, the First Years gathered for their Flight lesson on the front lawn of Glitterwings, with the great tree rising up behind them.

'Now then,' said Mrs Lightwing, zipping to and fro in front of the long line of fairies. 'The thing to remember about flying is that it's all about instinct. Instinct!'

Twink looked quickly around her, frowning. No one else seemed confused. But her father had always told her not to be embarrassed about asking questions, so she raised her hand.

'Yes?' said Mrs Lightwing, hovering in front of her.

'What does instinct mean?' asked Twink.

Mrs Lightwing opened her mouth, but before she could answer a voice hissed, 'Fancy not knowing that!'

Mariella! Twink felt her cheeks colour. Beside her, Sooze made a face and rolled her eyes.

Mrs Lightwing glared at Mariella and flew quickly over to her. 'What does it mean, then?' she barked. 'Speak loudly, so we can all hear!'

Mariella smirked, brushing silvery-green hair out of her eyes. 'It means talent. Flying's all about having talent, and I know *I'm* going to have lots of it, because –'

'Incorrect!' boomed Mrs Lightwing, her wings

fluttering so hard that she shot up several centimetres in the air. 'It's not about talent at all, you silly girl!'

Mariella coloured up, scowling, as the other fairies snickered.

'Instinct is doing something without thinking about it,' Mrs Lightwing went on. 'Fairies are meant to fly, and you'll all fly beautifully if you just relax and let your wings do the thinking for you!'

'Why do we need flying lessons, then?' asked Sooze.

Mrs Lightwing almost smiled. 'Because you need to learn certain skills to get the most out of your wingwork. Watch!'

With that, she shot straight up in the air. As the girls watched, open-mouthed, she did a series of loop-the-loops over their heads, turning and twisting in a sparkling blur. A few barrel rolls and back flips later, and she dived straight down at the line of girls, pulling out at the last moment to land neatly in front of them.

The First Years burst into applause. Mrs

Lightwing smoothed her sky-blue hair, trying to hide her smile.

'You get the idea,' she said sternly. 'Now then – let's get the fairy dust out and get you girls flying!'

'About time!' whispered Sooze. She and Twink smiled at each other and clutched hands.

Mrs Lightwing and an assistant – a serious-looking girl from one of the upper years – made their way down the long line of girls. As each fairy closed her eyes, there was a sudden sparkling of gold and pink in the air, and then squeals of delight.

'Stay on the ground, please!' ordered Mrs Lightwing. 'No flying just yet!'

Finally it was Twink's turn. She held her breath as Mrs Lightwing's assistant carefully measured out the fairy dust in a ladybird shell. The dust twinkled and shimmered.

'Eyes closed,' said Mrs Lightwing, taking the shell.

Twink screwed her eyes shut, holding her breath. There was a singing sound, like tiny silvery chimes – and then the most wonderful, laughing sensation burst through her wings!

'Oh!' she cried, her eyes flying open. 'I can feel it!'

'Stay on the ground,' Mrs Lightwing repeated firmly.

Once all the girls had been dusted, Mrs Lightwing flew in front of them, gazing up and down the long line of excited fairies.

'Right!' she said. 'We're going to learn the basics this morning, so we can get you girls flying to your classes and branches. When I give the signal, I want you to all *slowly* rise up in the air until I say stop. Ready?'

Yes! thought Twink. Her wings trembled in anticipation.

'Rise!' cried Mrs Lightwing.

Twink's wings beat wildly and, before she knew it, she had shot up several feet in the air. 'Eek!' she screamed as the ground grew smaller beneath her. The world swung crazily, and she screamed again. This was worse than being on a bird!

'Slowly!' said Mrs Lightwing, appearing beside her. 'Deep, controlled wing strokes!'

'I can't!' yelled Twink. Her wings had a life of

their own, flapping and fluttering. She looked down again and saw the class, back on the lawn, gaping up at her. Their faces were as tiny as poppy seeds. A coldness swept over Twink. Oh, wasps! She was up in the air, with nothing but her wings to support her!

All at once her wings froze. The world went black, and Twink plummeted towards the ground.

When she came to, she was lying on the grass with Mrs Lightwing leaning over her, frowning and gently slapping her hands.

'Great Mab, girl,' she said when she saw Twink's eyes open. 'I've never seen a fairy do that in all my years of teaching! I had to do some fancy flying to catch you before you hit the ground, I can tell you that!'

She helped Twink stand up. Embarrassment blazed through her when she saw that the entire first-year class stood staring at her.

'What did I say about talent?' Twink heard Mariella whisper to Lola. The two of them tittered. Twink's ears burned.

'Come on, then, have another go,' said Mrs Lightwing.

Twink's stomach turned. 'Now?' she gasped.

'Of course now!' snapped the teacher. 'Can't let you get wing fright, can we? Straight up in the air again, that's the thing! Get back in line; we'll all have another go.'

Shakily, Twink rejoined the other girls. Sooze leaned towards her and whispered, 'You went higher than anyone! What did you get so scared for? It looked great!'

Twink remembered the icy feeling that had gripped her wings, and swallowed hard. Mrs Lightwing wasn't really going to make her do this again, was she?

But she was. 'Rise!' she shouted, hovering with her hands on her hips.

Slowly, thought Twink fervently. *SLOWLY!* Clenching her fists, she concentrated on moving her wings just a little bit at a time. A few seconds later, she realised that she was the only fairy still on the ground.

Mrs Lightwing sighed. 'Stop and hover, everyone,' she called.

The rest of the First Years fluttered in the air, peering down at her. Twink stood by herself, slowly opening and closing her wings. Her cheeks were on fire.

Mrs Lightwing landed in front of Twink, regarding her carefully. 'You're thinking too much, my girl,' she said. 'Relax! Let your wings do the work for you!'

Twink gulped. She had never felt less relaxed in her life.

'Come on, now, try again,' said Mrs Lightwing. 'When I say *rise*, you –'

WHOOSH! Twink's wings took off of their own accord, zooming her straight up in the air. A few of the hovering fairies screamed and darted out of her way.

'Aagh!' shrieked Twink, swooping wildly about. 'Help, I can't stop!' She shot towards Glitterwings. The great tree seemed to spin in front of her, branches flailing.

'Slow down!' bawled Mrs Lightwing behind her. 'STEER!'

Twink clapped her hands over her eyes, expecting at any moment to crash into the school. Icy terror swept over her. All at once her wings froze again. A moment later, she was falling towards the ground.

This time when she came to, Mrs Lightwing looked shaken. Her sky-blue hair hung in messy strands about her face.

'I barely caught you that time!' she gasped. 'I think you've had enough flying for today.'

Twink struggled to sit up. 'But I need to learn

how to fly like the others!' she cried. She fought to hold back tears.

'Not today,' said Mrs Lightwing firmly, tucking her hair back into place. 'You just sit there and rest while I go on with the lesson. We'll get you flying tomorrow.' Twink saw a worried look flicker across her teacher's face. 'Or . . . well, as soon as we can, anyway.'

As the other fairies got back into line, Sooze skimmed quickly over to Twink. 'Don't worry, Opposite, you'll get it soon!' she said. 'I bet you'll be better than any of us!'

She flew off again, her pink wings glinting in the sunlight. She already looked like a natural, thought Twink sadly. Everyone did, except for her.

'Ready, and . . . rise!' called Mrs Lightwing.

Her heart heavy, Twink sat in the grass and watched the rest of the First Years learn to bank, turn and land. Mrs Lightwing encouraged them to fly a little higher with each exercise, so that by the end of the lesson, the girls were dipping and twirling high over Twink's head.

She could hear Sooze laughing, chatting with some of the other fairies as they buzzed about. Mariella flew with her nose stuck in the air, executing very grand banks and turns. With one of them, she and Lola dived straight past Twink, who had to duck to avoid being hit.

'Oh, sorry!' said Mariella loudly. 'We didn't see you *sitting* there.'

'Yeah, sorry,' echoed Lola with a smirk. The two fairies snickered as they flew away.

Twink flushed, glaring after them. *Never mind*, she thought, leaning against a dandelion stalk and hugging her knees. *I'll learn how to fly tomorrow.* Her lavender wings opened and shut in the sunlight, as though promising to behave.

But at the thought of flying again, something inside Twink shivered. What if . . . what if she never learned how? She'd be the only fairy in the school still riding a bird!

Twink swallowed hard. *No*, she thought fiercely. *I'll get it tomorrow. I will!*

Chapter Three

But Twink didn't learn to fly the next day, or even the day after that. A week went by, and Twink was the only fairy at Glitterwings Academy who remained land-locked. A dozen times a day, the great hollow trunk was filled with a rainbow of flying fairies, darting and swooping their way to class – and one red-cheeked fairy clinging to a bird.

The other fairies tried to pretend they didn't notice Twink, but they whispered about her once she passed. 'There must be something wrong with her,' Twink heard a green-haired Fourth Year hiss to a friend. 'Do you think they'll even let her stay at school?'

Twink's pointed ears burned as she blinked back tears.

'Don't mind her,' said Sooze, flying by her side. 'If they'll let an idiot like her stay, I'm sure they'll let you!'

This wasn't exactly comforting, and Twink felt very glum as she flew with the rest of Daffodil Branch to a Dance lesson. Dance classes were held outside, in a fairy ring of mushrooms that grew near the wood.

'Quickly, quickly!' called Madame Brightfoot, clapping her hands and hovering above the ground. 'We have much to do today!'

Twink slid off her bird's back and patted his wing. The bird squad had all been sent home, except for this one bright-eyed tit called Sunny. And even though Twink's heart still leapt in her throat when-ever she left the ground, she and Sunny had become great friends. It wasn't *his* fault that everyone was whispering about her.

'My favourite class!' grinned Sooze as she landed lightly beside Twink. She leaned close, her violet eyes sparkling. 'And I've got a surprise for Madame, wait and see!'

Twink's spirits lifted. Sooze had a voracious appetite for tricks and pranks. Just the day before, she had swapped Mrs Hover's bag of fairy dust for one of ordinary dust, and then innocently pointed out that her daffodil dress needed mending.

'Well, I never!' a red-faced Mrs Hover had exclaimed as she sprinkled more and more dust on the stubborn tear. 'Whatever's wrong with the stuff?' Twink and the others had had to bite their lips to keep from exploding with laughter.

Now Twink formed a circle with the rest of Daffodil Branch, with Madame Brightfoot in the centre. Madame had dramatic red wings, and wore shimmering cobweb dresses with tiny sparkling stones on them.

'Join hands and spread your wings!' she cried. Her bright purple hair was piled atop her head, with wispy bits falling down here and there.

The fairies joined hands, wings touching. From above, they looked like a many-petalled flower.

'Now,' said Madame, patting her hair. 'All fairies love to dance, but not all dances are just for fun. Some dances are magical, and this dance I'm about to teach you is a very important one. If you do it correctly, you shall be able to hear what the wood is thinking!'

Excitement rippled through the group. The fairies looked at each other, eyes shining.

Mariella tossed her head. 'I'm sure I've done this before,' she said. 'My old school was very advanced. We used to hear what the wood was thinking all the time.'

I bet it was wishing that you'd go away, thought Twink.

'Three steps to the right!' called Madame, throwing her arms wide and fluttering in the air. 'Dip and turn, close your wings and open them!'

The fairies began to dance, carefully following Madame's instructions. Twink murmured the steps to herself as Madame called them out. 'Two steps

left . . . twirl in place . . .'

It was such a lovely dance! And suddenly Twink saw that magic was beginning to gather around them, like sparkling flakes of sunshine. She caught her breath in delight.

'Now you all fly up together, one-two-three wing beats, and join hands in the air!' cried Madame.

Oh, no! Twink's heart fell into her pixie boots. The rest of the circle took to the air like butterflies, leaving her red-faced on the ground. The flakes of sunshine vanished with little popping sounds as the spell broke.

'What is this?' called Madame. 'You have ruined the dance! Why are you not in the air?'

'I'm – I'm sorry, Madame,' stammered Twink. 'It's just that –'

'She can't fly,' broke in Mariella. She and Lola snickered.

'Oh! You are *that* girl,' said Madame. 'I had forgotten. Ah. Well – you shall just have to hop for now, instead of flying. *Pretend* to fly. We shall not hear the wood's thoughts today, but you shall all learn the steps.'

Miserably, Twink joined hands with the others as the dance began again. No one said a word to her, not even Sooze. She was sure they all blamed her for ruining the dance.

'Now fly!' said Madame. Feeling like an idiot, Twink hopped in place as the others lifted up in the air. She could hear Mariella and Lola laughing, and she grit her teeth. She was *not* going to let them get to her.

'Madame!' cried Sooze suddenly. 'What's that on

your shoulder?'

'You bad fairy, you have ruined the dance also!' said Madame, exasperated. 'What is this you are saying? What about my shoulder?'

'There's a – a *thing* on it,' said Sooze, wide-eyed and innocent. The fairies all landed, clustering about Madame. Twink pressed her lips together to keep from shouting with laughter. There was a fat green glow-worm nestled on Madame's shoulder, purring gently.

'Oh! Get it off! Get away from me, you glow-thing!' shrieked Madame, swatting at her shoulder. The glow-worm nuzzled Madame's neck, humming with pleasure.

'I think he likes you, Madame,' said Pix, her voice wobbling with laughter.

'But I do not like it! Horrid things, they should stay in lamps!' Madame tried to scrape the worm off, but it clung to her like a tiny owl.

'Maybe you should go and see Matron,' said Sooze, her violet eyes wide. 'He seems really attached to you.'

'I shall! I shall! Class dismissed!' And Madame flew quickly away towards Glitterwings, the affectionate glow-worm still cuddled on her shoulder.

Mariella sniffed. 'I think *you* had something to do with that,' she said to Sooze. 'I've never seen a glow-worm do that before!'

'Me? How could I?' demanded Sooze. 'We don't learn power spells until third year.'

Mariella scowled, but had no answer for this. 'Come on, Lola,' she snapped. The two fairies flew haughtily away.

The rest of Daffodil Branch pressed around Sooze. 'How did you do it?' gasped Twink. 'I've never seen anything so funny!'

Sooze grinned, fluttering her wings. 'My sister gave me some fairy dust with a love spell cast on it. It wears off after a few minutes – by the time Madame gets to Matron, that worm won't care about her in the least!'

The fairies howled with laughter, imagining it. Even Bimi was smiling. 'Madame will think she's gone mad!' cried a yellow-haired fairy called Zena.

'Sooze, you're brilliant!'

Twink laughed with the others, glad of the chance to forget about not being able to fly. But once the merriment died down, Pix looked thoughtfully at her.

'Twink, it's really too bad that you still can't fly,' she said. 'I wonder if there's anything we can do to help you?'

Twink made a face. 'Mrs Lightwing says I just need to relax, but I can't seem to do it.' She tried not to let the others see how much this bothered her. Every night, she had nightmares about flying

Pix

that turned her wings cold.

'Maybe there's something she hasn't thought of,' said Pix. 'I think I'll fly to the library after dinner and do some research.'

Twink's heart lifted. 'Oh, Pix, would you?' she cried. Everyone already knew that Pix was the cleverest fairy in their year. If anyone could figure out a solution, she could!

Pix nodded seriously, tucking a strand of short red hair behind her ear. 'Yes, of course. It's not just for you – it'll be wonderful for all of us when you can fly!'

The first-year Common Branch was a cosy, moss-carpeted space with spotted mushrooms for seats, and a ring of fire rocks at its centre – enchanted stones that glowed hot in the winter and cool in the summer. Normally in the evenings the branch was filled with chattering fairies doing their homework, but that night everyone crowded around Pix.

'Well? Have you found anything out yet?' asked Sooze.

'A few things,' said Pix. She opened a petal book

and flipped through its pages. 'Twink, you're not the first fairy who couldn't fly. There was another one called Agnes Leadwing back in 1047. *She* couldn't fly, either.'

'What happened to her?' asked Twink eagerly.

'Well . . .' Pix rubbed her nose. 'Actually, she never did learn how to fly. She had to have a special mouse cart made for her, and she rode around in that all her life.'

'Oh,' whispered Twink.

Sooze made a face. 'Pix, that doesn't help at all! Didn't you find out anything useful?'

Pix flushed and put the petal book away. 'I tried. There's just not a lot in the library about it. *Every* fairy can fly.'

'Except Twink,' sniffed Mariella, listening in from the edge of the group. 'Really, I don't know why you're all bothering. It's obvious that there's something wrong with her.'

'There is not!' cried Twink. 'I'll be able to fly just as well as you soon, wait and see!'

'*No* one can fly as well as Mariella,' said Lola

primly. 'She's the best of anybody.'

'They should send you home,' continued Mariella, narrowing her eyes at Twink. 'You're holding the whole year back. We can't even listen to the wood because of you!'

Twink's throat tightened. She couldn't answer.

Sooze took a step forward, her pink wings opening and shutting rapidly. 'I think you should just be quiet now,' she said in a low voice. 'We're all behind Twink, even if *you* aren't.'

The Common Branch held its breath, waiting to see what Mariella would do. The pointed-faced fairy flushed and looked away.

'I'm going to bed now,' she announced. 'I've had enough of this.' And she flounced off, with Lola fluttering after her.

'Phew!' said Zena. 'We shan't see *her* again anytime soon.'

'Good,' said Sooze. 'Who wants to!'

'Thanks,' Twink said shyly to everyone. 'But . . . I suppose she's right, really. Maybe I should just go home.' She swallowed hard at the thought of telling her parents she couldn't fly. She had been pretending in her letters home that everything was fine.

'Don't you dare,' said Bimi unexpectedly. They all turned and looked at the normally quiet fairy in surprise. Her pretty cheeks reddened. 'Well, you can't let *Mariella* chase you off, can you? It would just be too sickening!'

'She's right,' Pix nodded. 'We've got to think of something to help you, Twink.'

'I know!' said Sooze suddenly, lifting off the ground in her excitement. 'What about the fairy dust? Maybe you didn't have enough sprinkled on you!'

Twink gasped as hope flickered through her. 'Do you think that's it?'

'Why not?' said Sooze. 'What else could it be?'

Pix shook her head. 'She got the same fairy dust as the rest of us, and *we* can all fly. I don't think that's it.'

Sooze landed with a thump. 'Oh, don't be such a wet leaf, Pix! It's worth asking Mrs Lightwing about it, isn't it?' She grinned at Twink. 'We'll do it tomorrow. I bet you'll be flying by lunchtime!'

Chapter
Four

'No,' said Mrs Lightwing.

'But –' started Twink.

Mrs Lightwing shook her blue head firmly. 'I'm sorry to disappoint you, but there wasn't anything wrong with the fairy dust. You *can* fly, Twink – you just get frightened and can't control it. See me after school today; I think it's time I gave you some extra help.' And she flew off without even a backwards look.

They were in the Great Branch, where the school was having breakfast. Twink sat down and looked

glumly at her cup of nectar. She saw Mariella whisper something to Lola, and winced as they giggled.

'I told you,' said Pix sympathetically. 'Never mind, we'll work something else out.'

'Well, I still think we should at least try it,' said Sooze. 'Winn told me that they once got a bad batch of fairy dust in a Creature Kindness class, and a caterpillar turned into a frog! If just one flake isn't right, everything can go wrong.'

Twink stared at her. 'But how can we try it? Mrs Lightwing said –'

Sooze shrugged. 'I'll get some more fairy dust from Winn. She uses it in her lessons. Just leave it to me!'

Pix let out a breath. 'Sooze, I don't think –'

A hush fell over the Great Branch. Looking around, Twink saw that Miss Shimmery had flown on to the raised platform.

'Good morning!' called the HeadFairy. 'I have some very exciting news. As our old girls know, each year Glitterwings Academy puts on an exhibition for your parents. Well, this year it's going to come early. We're going to have a special Flying Exhibition at the end of this term! All of your parents are invited, and I know that you'll make me very proud.'

Twink froze in horror as the Great Branch erupted in excited whispers. Oh, no! What would her parents think when they saw her on the ground? Then she remembered that they were going to be away at the end of term, and her wings sagged in relief. Even so, it was still awful. She'd be humiliated in front of everyone!

Sooze didn't seem to notice the look on Twink's face. She was busy chattering away to a silver-haired fairy called Sili. 'What a glimmery idea! Usually the exhibitions are totally boring. But *this* – we can really show off and have some fun!'

Twink clutched Sooze's arm. 'Sooze, you won't forget about the fairy dust, will you?' she whispered. 'It's important!'

Sooze shook her head. 'Don't worry, I won't forget,' she whispered back.

Miss Shimmery held up her hands. 'Quiet, please! Now, I know that I can depend upon every fairy in this school to make our exhibition an outstanding occasion.' She folded her rainbow-coloured wings behind her back. 'Let's all sing the Glitterwings song.' From behind her, a small band of crickets leapt into place, tuning up their legs like violins.

Trying not to look as worried as she felt, Twink rose with the others, opening and closing her wings in time to the music as they sang.

Oh, Glitterwings, dear Glitterwings
Beloved oak tree scho-ool.
Good fairy fun for everyone,
That is our fairy ru-ule.
Our teachers wise,
Their magic strong,
With all our friends,
We can't go wrong.
Oh, Glitterwings, dear Glitterwings
Beloved oak tree scho-ool.

As the day went on, Twink wasn't at all sure that Sooze would remember the fairy dust. The whole school was buzzing about the Flying Exhibition, and Sooze seemed more excited than anyone. She darted ahead of Twink and Sunny as they flew to their Flower Power class, doing somersaults in the air with Sili and Zena.

'Look at us! We'll be the stars of the show!' she cried.

The excitement continued in class, with buzzing whispers filling the branch.

'Girls, pay attention!' said Miss Petal. 'We're about to do a practical demonstration.' She flew to a wooden cupboard and brought out a small acorn pot. A tiny drooping daisy grew in it, its leaves limp and sad-looking.

'Now then,' said Miss Petal, putting the flower on a table. 'If a daisy is poorly, what do you do?'

Twink shifted on her mushroom seat. Usually Pix was the first to wave her hand in the air, but today, like all the others, she was gazing out of the window.

'Look, the Second Years are practising already,' someone muttered. 'We want to make sure we do better than *them*.'

'Girls!' called Miss Petal, rapping the table with her hand. 'I know that flowers don't take part in flying exhibitions, but can we please pay some attention to them anyway?'

The whispers quietened somewhat as the class reluctantly settled down.

'All right, now watch,' said Miss Petal. 'You just put your hands on the flower, and you send it cheerful thoughts.'

Twink watched as Miss Petal rested her fingertips on the daisy's leaves and shut her eyes. Almost instantly the flower perked up, lifting its head until it looked bright and strong.

Miss Petal stepped back with a wide smile. 'There, you see? The technique varies a bit for more complicated flowers, like roses and orchids, but for many of them, you can just use cheerful thoughts to heal them.'

Twink glanced around her. If Miss Petal had expected her class to be impressed, she must be disappointed! Most of the others were already gazing out of the window again, dreaming of flying.

Miss Petal sighed and put the flower away. 'All right, everyone, open your books.'

It was even worse in Flight class. When Twink arrived at the flying field, everyone had already been split into teams of three. Mrs Lightwing flew overhead, bellowing orders.

'Right, teams, work on your barrel rolls – all together, now! Nice, precise wingwork!'

Sooze was in a team with Sili and Zena. Jealousy pricked Twink as the three of them laughed

together. She shook herself.

I'm being silly. She's still my best friend, even if she likes Sili and Zena too!

Finally Mrs Lightwing noticed Twink, and landed in front of her. 'We'll have those extra lessons this afternoon, Twink – but meanwhile, watch the others, and notice their technique. Especially Mariella; she's got it down pat. Look at her go!'

Annoyingly, it was true: Mariella was twisting and turning with the greatest of ease, flipping about in the air like a fish in water. Twink could see the smirk on her face as Lola and Bimi struggled to keep up with her. *Poor Bimi,* thought Twink. *Imagine having to fly with Mariella!*

But at least she could fly. 'Mrs Lightwing, what am I going to do?' burst out Twink.

The Flight mistress patted her arm. 'Don't you worry,' she said staunchly. 'We'll get you flying yet!'

But Twink thought Mrs Lightwing looked worried as she flew away. She thought of Agnes Leadwing and her mouse carriage, and swallowed hard.

* * *

The different flying teams clustered together in the Common Branch that night, making plans. 'Let's do some extra practice tomorrow!' suggested Zena.

Twink watched as Sooze fluttered her wings in agreement. 'Glimmery! We'll do some loop-the-loops, and give Mrs Lightwing a real surprise!'

It was obvious that she had forgotten all about the fairy dust. Twink looked away. She was sitting alone at one of the mushroom desks with her Flower Power homework: a drooping daisy that needed a cheering-up spell.

Taking a deep breath, Twink put her hands on the flower's leaves and tried to imitate Miss Petal, sending the daisy cheerful thoughts as hard as she could. But her thoughts must not have been very cheerful, and the daisy drooped even further. Oh, great! Twink let out a heavy sigh.

Her extra flying lesson with Mrs Lightwing that afternoon had been a complete disaster. Twink had shot straight up in the air again and got hopelessly tangled in the lower branches of Glitterwings. It had taken Mrs Lightwing and two of the Sixth Years

almost an hour to get her down again. Twink's cheeks flamed at the memory.

It's all right for Sooze, she thought crossly, watching the lavender-haired fairy laugh with Sili and Zena. *She's not the one who can't fly!*

Then she felt guilty. Sooze was a sparkly, wonderful friend. Why shouldn't she be looking forward to the exhibition?

Because I'm dreading it, answered a tiny voice inside of her. Wouldn't a *real* friend notice how Twink was feeling? Twink's wings slumped, and she pushed the flower away. It would just have to cheer up without her, somehow.

Suddenly Sooze appeared at her side, violet eyes shining. 'What are you doing hiding over here, Opposite? I've got something for you!'

Twink scrambled from her seat. 'You mean –'

Sooze pulled a small pouch from her petal bag. 'Fairy dust,' she announced proudly. 'Winn gave me a good pinch of it. We'll have you flying properly in no time!'

Happiness burst through Twink. Sooze *did* care

how she was feeling after all. She had been such a wasp brain to doubt her!

Sooze pulled at Twink's arm. 'Let's test it out over here, in front of the fire rocks where there's a bit of room. Come on, everyone, clear a space!' The first-year fairies all crowded to one side, murmuring excitedly.

'Good luck, Twink!' cried Sili. 'We've got our wings crossed for you!'

'You're going to do it here in the Common Branch?' said Pix doubtfully.

'Why not?' said Sooze, positioning Twink on the moss carpet. 'We all want to see Twink fly, don't we?'

'We're not allowed to fly in here, though,' pointed out Pix.

'I'll only fly a little bit,' promised Twink. She bounced on her tiptoes, excitement tingling through her.

'But you can't control it, that's the problem!' Pix flapped her yellow wings in exasperation. 'Sooze, I really don't think this is a good idea – '

Sooze ignored her. Reaching into the pouch, she scooped out a glistening handful of fairy dust. 'Twink, are you ready?'

Twink nodded, and screwed her eyes up hard. *Please work, please, please!* she begged silently.

The tinkling of chimes whispered through the air again as Sooze threw the dust on her. The same wonderful feeling as before rushed through Twink, and she gasped. Had it worked? She cracked an eye open cautiously, her heart beating hard.

'Well, how do you feel?' demanded Sooze. 'Oh, I

bet it worked, you look all flushed!' She shot a few inches off the floor, bouncing up and down in the air. 'Come on, Twink, fly! You can do it now, I know you can!'

Twink took a deep breath. Almost everyone in the first year stood to one side, watching her. At least Mariella and Lola weren't there!

'What are you waiting for?' demanded Sooze, hovering above her.

'Nothing!' Twink grit her teeth, concentrating hard . . . and then suddenly *SWOOSHED* up into the air.

'Agh!' she cried, arms and legs flailing. She banged wildly about the room, knocking drawings off the wall and overturning a mug of nectar. Sooze shrieked and ducked out of her way.

Crack! Twink slammed into the ceiling at full speed. She fell back to the floor, where she lay in a crumpled heap.

'Are you all right?' cried Zena. She and Pix rushed to Twink's side, helping her up.

'Ooohh . . . that hurt,' moaned Twink.

Sooze landed beside her. 'Try again,' she suggested. 'Come on, do it now before you lose your nerve!'

Twink shook her head, tears stinging at her eyes. 'Didn't you see me? I almost went through the ceiling! It's hopeless! I'll never fly.'

'Of course you will!' Sooze patted her shoulder. 'Twink, *all* fairies can fly.'

'Agnes Leadwing couldn't,' whispered Twink.

Silence fell over the Common Branch. Pix cleared her throat. 'Well . . . the books think that maybe she was a special case –'

'I don't want to hear another word about that stupid Agnes!' Sooze rubbed a pink wing against Twink's lavender one. 'You'll learn to fly, and that's the end of it.'

Pix nodded eagerly. 'I'll think of something, Twink, I promise!'

Twink managed a smile. 'Really?'

'Of course!' cried Sooze. 'Twink, you *have* to learn to fly; you're missing out on too much fun other-wise.' She pulled Twink to her feet. 'Like the Flying

Exhibition, for instance! You don't want to stay on the ground for it, do you? We have to get you flying!'

Chapter Five

Nobody, though, had any bright ideas in the weeks that followed, and Twink stayed on the ground. Mrs Lightwing kept giving Twink extra lessons, but nothing the Flight mistress tried seemed to work.

'Relax!' she kept ordering. 'You're thinking too much, my girl. Don't think, just fly!' And Twink would clench her fists, mutter *don't think, don't think* to herself – and promptly fly into the tree again.

Meanwhile the flying teams practised every day, swooping high overhead during Flight class. Twink sat on the ground watching them, trying to be a

good sport and not to feel too sorry for herself.

'Go, Sooze!' she cheered as her friend's team looped the loop in perfect formation.

Sooze grinned and waved as they flew past. 'That is *so* much fun!' she called.

Twink watched as Sooze's team zoomed over the pond at the far end of the field, scattering blue and green dragonflies as they went. One of the insects landed on a bulrush, beating its bright wings. The reed dipped down close to the ground, springing up again when the dragonfly flew away.

Twink groaned despite herself. Even the dragon-flies flew better than she did!

Mrs Lightwing hovered up above, shouting instructions to the teams. 'Now just carry on prac-tising for a bit,' she bellowed through cupped hands. Gracefully going into a dive, she skimmed through the air and landed on the ground beside Twink.

'Well now, my girl,' she said, patting her blue hair into place. 'I think the time has come to work out what you're doing for the exhibition, don't you? It's

only a week away now.'

Twink blinked. 'But how can I do anything? I can't fly.'

'You can't fly *yet*,' corrected Mrs Lightwing with a frown. 'But you'll still be taking part in the exhibition. I've a very important part in mind for you.'

'You do?' gasped Twink.

Mrs Lightwing nodded. 'I've been talking to Madame Brightfoot, and we have just the thing. While the teams are flying, you're going to do a special dance on the ground.'

A dance on the ground? Twink's cheeks caught fire as she imagined it.

'Do I have to?' she blurted.

'Now, none of that!' said Mrs Lightwing sternly. 'We can't have you not taking part with the rest of your year, can we?'

Twink didn't see why not. She shrugged, looking down.

The Flight mistress tipped up Twink's chin with a firm finger. 'I don't want you feeling sorry for yourself, my girl. Where's your Glitterwings spirit? You'll do the dance Madame Brightfoot assigns you, and you'll do it as well as you possibly can!' Mrs Lightwing took to the air in a flurry of wings. A moment later she was shouting instructions to the teams again.

Twink clapped her wings together, blinking back tears. A dance! A stupid little dance on the ground while everyone else flew!

Sunny hopped over from where he had been pecking for worms, and nudged her arm with a concerned chirp. Twink pressed her hot cheek against the smooth feathers of his wing, wiping her tears away.

'Oh, Sunny,' she muttered. 'I'll feel like such an idiot! In front of the whole school, too. I'm *so* glad my parents won't be there – that would make everything ten times worse!'

Mariella's team swooped past. 'Dearie me, there's trouble on the ground,' called Mariella. 'Poor Twink, are you upset that you can't do *this*?'

Quick as a hummingbird, Mariella zoomed into a loop-the-loop. Lola followed, snickering wildly. Only Bimi stayed behind. Colouring up, she crossed her arms over her chest and fluttered in place, not looking at Twink.

Twink glared up at Mariella. *Why* couldn't she just leave her alone?

Just then Lola came out of her loop, flying wildly and much too fast. *Thump!* She crashed straight into Bimi.

'Oh!' shrieked Lola as she fell.

Twink sprang to help without thinking, sprinting across the grass. She reached the struggling fairy moments before she landed, cushioning her fall with her arms.

'Oomf!' grunted Twink as they thudded to the ground together. She slowly sat up, rubbing her head. 'Are you all right?'

Lola looked dazed. 'I – I think so. I got a wing cramp when I crashed into Bimi, that's all.'

'Is it better now?' Twink helped Lola to her feet.

Lola fluttered her pale blue wings, peering behind her. She nodded, and looked shyly at Twink. 'Um – that was – I mean, you really –'

Mariella landed beside them, her pointed face flushed. She took Lola's arm. 'How nice that we have such an efficient *ground crew*,' she said loudly, tossing her silvery-green hair. 'Isn't it, Lola?'

She scowled at Lola, who swallowed hard. 'Oh, yes! Yes, it is!'

'It's really just as well you can't fly,' said Mariella, smirking at Twink. 'We need you on the ground!'

She took off in a rush of wings, with Lola following behind her. Twink glared after them. *Oh!* Couldn't Mariella even say *one* nice thing to her?

Glancing up, she saw Bimi hovering a few inches away.

'What do you want?' she asked crossly.

The pretty fairy's cheeks blazed. 'I just – oh, Twink, I'm sorry! She's so –'

'Teams together now!' bellowed Mrs Lightwing, swooping past and clapping her hands. 'Quickly, I want to do a full run-through.'

Bimi's face was like a bright red poppy flower. She flew slowly away, looking back over her shoulder. Faintly, Twink could hear Sooze laughing with Sili

and Zena. Nobody else had even noticed what happened.

Twink perched on a dandelion leaf with her chin cupped in her hands. A ladybird trundled down the flower's stalk, and Twink patted it glumly on the head.

'You know, ladybird . . . I'm not enjoying school as much as I thought I would.'

Before dinner that evening, the school butterflies fluttered into the Great Branch with letters and packages from home. A yellow butterfly hovered gracefully above Twink, dropping a rolled-up rose petal into her lap.

'Ooh, look, Mum's sent me a new leaf pad,' said Sooze beside her, tearing open a package. 'I suppose Winn told her I lost my old one!'

'You *always* lose things,' pointed out Twink with a grin. She unrolled the pink petal curiously.

Dear Twink, said the shimmering silver ink.

Your father and I were so disappointed at the thought of missing your Flying Exhibition that we've

decided not to go to the Fairy Medics' Meeting after all. We'll be at Glitterwings Academy with all the other parents and families, and we're going to bring Teena along, too. She's so excited she can hardly keep still!

Don't be nervous about the exhibition, Twink. Just do your best and we'll be as proud of you as we always are. See you soon!

Love from,

Mum and Dad

'Oh, no!' gasped Twink. She glanced quickly at Sooze, but her friend was chattering away to Sili and Zena about barrel rolls.

'Twink, are you OK? What's wrong?' asked Bimi from across the table.

Dropping the letter, Twink buried her head in her hands with a groan. 'Oh, nothing. Just the worst thing ever!'

'Let's think about this logically,' said Pix. 'Twink, *why* can't you fly?' They were all gathered in the Common Branch, sitting perched on mushrooms and on the mossy carpet.

'I don't know,' said Twink. 'Mrs Lightwing says I think too much. She says flying should be instinctive, but that I worry about it so much that my wings get all tangled up.'

She tried to sound calm, but her heart was racing. What in the world was she going to do? She couldn't let her parents down in front of everyone. They were so proud of her! She *had* to learn to fly before the exhibition.

Pix nodded. 'So if we're going to get you flying by the time your parents get here, we need to help you not to think. You've got to be in a situation where you *have* to fly, and don't have time to worry about it!'

'I know!' said Sooze with a wicked smile. 'Let's push her off a ledge!'

Twink tried to laugh with the others, but it didn't seem very funny. Trust Sooze to make a joke out of it!

'Hang on!' said Pix, her eyes widening. 'Sooze, I think you might be on to something.'

'Of course I am,' grinned Sooze. 'I'm a genius, didn't you know?'

'Sooze, stop messing around! It's really not a bad idea. If Twink were falling, somehow, so that she *had* to fly –' Pix tapped her chin, frowning. 'Come on, everyone, think!'

'Maybe . . . maybe we could build a fairy pyramid,' suggested Bimi. Her cheeks reddened as everyone looked at her. 'Out on the front lawn, I mean. And then Twink could climb to the top and jump off.'

'I don't know,' said Pix doubtfully. 'I think she'd still have too much time to think about being scared. It has to be *sudden*.'

All at once Twink saw the dragonfly from that morning again, landing on the bulrush and springing off it. Of course! Her wings trembled with excitement as she leapt to her feet.

'I've got it!' she cried. 'I've got the perfect idea!'

Chapter Six

'Twink, are you ready?' called Pix.

'Ready!' called Twink, clinging to the soft brown velvet of the bulrush. The greenish water of the pond lay underneath her. Looking down, she could see a wavering, wide-eyed reflection of herself.

I am not *going to be scared,* Twink told herself firmly. They had all discussed the plan over and over now, working out every detail. Nothing could go wrong.

'OK, everyone, bring it down!' ordered Pix, waving her arms. A flock of Daffodil Branch fairies

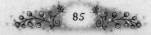

zoomed to the top of the bulrush. Grabbing hold of it from all directions, they pulled it towards the water until it lay flat.

Looking worried, Pix flew across to Twink. 'Are you *sure* you want to do this?' she whispered.

Twink nodded quickly before she could change her mind. 'Positive! We all agreed it's the best plan.'

'But if it doesn't work . . .'

Don't remind me! thought Twink. She straightened her wings. 'It's the only way! And it's not dangerous – I'll just fall in the water if you don't catch me.'

'All right,' sighed Pix. 'Now, Twink, on my count, you and the girls will all let go of the bulrush. It'll whip back up in the air, and you'll be aloft. And flying, with any luck!'

'About time, too,' added Sooze from her position a few inches away. 'All this planning was giving me a headache!'

Twink bit her lip. She knew Sooze had been bored these last few days, but she couldn't worry about that now.

Pix fluttered above the bulrush. 'All right,

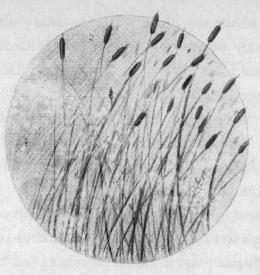

everyone, on my count!'

The fairies got into position.

'Three!' called Pix.

Twink's heart thumped like a woodpecker. She screwed her eyes shut.

'Two!'

Get ready to let go, she thought. *Get ready . . .*

'One –'

'WHAT IS THE MEANING OF THIS?' boomed a voice. 'GET THAT FAIRY DOWN FROM THERE THIS INSTANT!' Mrs Lightwing buzzed about the bulrush like an angry wasp. 'I do not *believe* what I am seeing!' she huffed. 'Twink, get down! Girls, fly that reed back into place and get on the ground!'

In no time at all, the bulrush was upright again and Twink was standing on the ground with the others. Mrs Lightwing hovered grimly in front of the shamefaced fairies.

'Do you have *any* idea what a dangerous, silly thing you were about to do?' she demanded.

The fairies gulped. Sooze slowly raised her hand. 'We were only trying to help –'

'HELP!' roared Mrs Lightwing. The fairies cringed. 'And what if she didn't fly, and landed in the water? Are you aware that a snapping turtle lives in that pond?'

A snapping turtle? Twink felt herself turn pale.

'I have NEVER, in all my years of teaching, seen such an *absolute disregard* of the school's rules –'

'Please, don't blame them!' cried Twink. 'I *asked* them to help! My parents are coming to the exhibition, and –'

The Flight mistress's wings were an angry white blur. 'That's no excuse, Twink! You and your classmates should have shown much better sense. You'll all miss your next free afternoon, and spend it writing two hundred lines: *I will not do silly, dangerous things!*'

'Oh, please, Mrs Lightwing, just make me do it, not the others, too!' burst out Twink.

Mrs Lightwing's eyes flashed. 'Do you want to make it five hundred lines?'

Twink bit her lip and fell silent.

'I thought not!' said Mrs Lightwing. 'The punishment stands. Now, get back to school this instant, all of you!'

Her tone left no room for argument. The Daffodil Branch fairies flew swiftly away, skimming over the grass.

Sunny chirped a friendly greeting as Twink climbed on to his back. The yellow and grey tit had been watching the proceedings with concern, and seemed relieved that Mrs Lightwing had turned up.

'I suppose it *was* sort of silly of us . . . but what

Sunny

else was I supposed to do?' muttered Twink, stroking his wing. 'And now we've all got to do two hundred lines! Everyone's going to hate me, and we didn't even get to see if the plan worked.'

Mrs Lightwing flew across as Twink gathered up her reins. 'Wait a moment, Twink. Did you say that your parents are coming?'

Twink nodded miserably. 'They don't know yet that I can't fly. I know I should have told them, but . . .' She trailed off.

A twitch of a smile lifted Mrs Lightwing's mouth. 'Well, I don't think turning yourself into a fairy catapult will solve things,' she said gruffly. 'What you need to do is get in the air without thinking about it, somehow! Now, get back to school, before I make it five hundred lines after all.'

To Twink's relief, no one seemed to blame her for the long afternoon spent writing lines – even though Mariella and Lola, who of course hadn't been part of the plan, gloated over their punishment at every opportunity. Once it was over, the rest of

the week sped past, until all at once it was the evening before the exhibition.

In the Common Branch, the first-year fairies drank fizzy nectar and chattered excitedly about the day to come. Twink tried to join in, but all she could think of was doing her dance on the ground while her parents watched.

Sooze nudged her with a wing. 'Opposite! What's the matter with you? You've hardly said a word all night!'

'I'm fine.' Twink managed a smile. She had promised herself that she wouldn't say anything else about flying to her friends, not after getting all of them in trouble.

'What is it?' pressed Sooze. 'Come on, you can tell me!'

Sudden tears pricked Twink's eyes. She took her friend's arm and led her to a quiet corner of the branch. 'Sooze, what am I going to do? My parents will be here tomorrow, and I still can't fly!'

Sooze blew out an impatient breath. 'Oh, Twink, not *that* again,' she groaned. 'You're no fun at all any more, you're always moaning about flying! Wasn't it bad enough that we all got writers' cramp the other day? What else do you want us to do?'

Twink felt like she had been slapped. 'But —'

'Just do your dance tomorrow! It won't be so bad. I'm going to go talk to Sili and Zena about our flight pattern.' Sooze fluttered off without a backward look.

Twink sank on to a bark bench and did her best not to cry. After all the times she had cheered Sooze's team on and listened to her talk about flying! She had tried so hard to be a good friend, but Sooze didn't even seem to have noticed.

'Hi,' said a voice.

Twink looked up. Bimi stood in front of her, holding two acorn-cap cups of fizzy nectar. 'Um . . . you left your nectar over there.' She held out one of the cups.

Twink wasn't in the mood for fizzy nectar any more, but she took it anyway. 'Thanks.'

Bimi sat down beside Twink. 'I overheard what just happened,' she said softly.

Twink fought back stinging tears. 'How could she say that?' she cried. 'I know I got everyone into trouble, but –'

'Twink, that wasn't your fault!' said Bimi. 'We all agreed to do it.'

Twink wiped her hand across her eyes. 'I thought she was my best friend, that's all. Bimi, do – do I really moan all the time?' She held her breath, waiting for the answer.

'Of course not!' said Bimi. 'I think you've been really brave about it. Wasps, if it were me, I'd be crying all the time! But Sooze is . . .' She trailed off, glancing across to where the lavender-haired fairy stood laughing and chatting with the others.

'What?' said Twink.

Bimi looked down at her nectar. 'Never mind.'

'I know what you were going to say,' said Twink slowly. 'Sooze is lots of fun, isn't she? But *having* fun is all she cares about. If something isn't fun, then – she doesn't want to know.' Twink managed a lop-sided smile. 'Even if it's happening to her Opposite.'

'Oh, Twink, it's really too bad!' burst out Bimi.

Twink put her nectar down and hugged her knees. 'Bimi, I *can't* do a dance on the ground while the rest of you perform, I just can't! My parents don't even know I can't fly! I'd rather break my leg and spend the exhibition in the infirmary.'

Bimi nodded. 'I don't blame you. But *that* wouldn't solve anything, would it?'

'At least I wouldn't be humiliated in front of my parents.' Twink rested her chin on her knees. 'They were so proud of me for getting into Glitterwings – and now this!'

'Have we really tried everything to get you flying?' asked Bimi. 'Maybe there's something we've over-looked. Tell me everything you can think of!'

So Twink told Bimi how Mrs Lightwing kept telling her to relax. 'She says that I need to get up in the air without thinking about it. But I don't know how to do that! And now we've tried everything, and there's nothing left to try!'

'Maybe not,' said Bimi, frowning softly.

Twink sat bolt upright. 'Have you thought of something?'

Bimi glanced quickly at her. 'No. We just – shouldn't give up hope, that's all.'

Twink made a face and slumped back against the wall. After a moment she smiled. 'You know, Bimi, when I first met you, I thought you were stuck-up. But you're not, you're really nice.'

'Stuck-up? Me?' Bimi's voice turned stiff.

Twink laughed. 'Yes, because you always sounded just like that! Like you didn't *really* want to be talking to anyone.'

Bimi looked like she had swallowed a chilli seed. 'I – I just – hate people staring at me, that's all,' she stammered. 'And people always do when I first meet them.'

'It's because you're so pretty,' said Twink. 'I thought you were the most beautiful fairy I had ever seen when I first met you! Your blue hair, and your gold and silver wings –'

'I hate them,' said Bimi glumly, drawing a pattern in the moss carpet with her pixie boot. 'I wish I were just normal, like everyone else. Do you remember what a fuss Mrs Hover made over me, that first day with our uniforms? I wanted to die!'

'But you know, I don't think about how pretty you are any more,' said Twink thoughtfully. 'You're just Bimi.'

'Really?' Bimi's blue eyes shone.

'Really!' Twink assured her. The two fairies smiled warmly at each other.

Twink glanced at Sooze again, and realised that she didn't mind so much now about what had happened. Maybe Sooze wasn't quite the wonderful friend she had thought . . . but she had a very good feeling about Bimi!

The two fairies sat talking until Twink began to yawn and stretch her wings. 'I'm going to bed,' she decided. 'I know it's still a few minutes until glow-worms out, but I'm so tired!'

After Twink left, Bimi sat alone for a few minutes, thinking hard. Finally she got up and joined the others. 'Pix, can I talk to you?' she asked, drawing the red-haired fairy away from the crowd.

Pix's normally serious face was flushed. 'Oh, Bimi,

isn't it glimmery? The exhibition is really almost here!'

'Yes, but I don't think Twink's too happy about it,' said Bimi in an undertone. 'Especially with her parents coming!'

Pix's face fell. 'Oh, poor Twink! I suppose we all forgot about her tonight. Wasps, how awful of us!'

'I think I might have an idea, though,' said Bimi. She quickly told Pix what she was thinking of. 'Only I'm not sure of the best way to do it,' she finished. 'Everyone in Daffy Branch would have to help for it to work.'

'Bimi, that's a fantastic idea!' said Pix excitedly. 'I think it could really work!'

'Me too,' said a voice behind them.

Bimi turned, and her eyes widened in surprise. Sooze was standing there.

'But I thought –' Bimi stopped, biting back the words.

Sooze reddened and fluttered her wings. 'I – I suppose I shouldn't have got so cross with Twink,' she said awkwardly. 'I was just feeling bored of it all, but I really do want to help. All right?'

Bimi smiled at the sheepish fairy. 'Sooze, that's glimmery! Of course you can help!' Privately, though, Bimi wondered how long it would be before Sooze got bored again!

'Everyone else will want to help, too, I'm sure of it,' said Pix. 'And I don't see how we can get in trouble this time, either. We're just doing what Mrs Lightwing said!'

Suddenly a dreadful thought came to Bimi. 'Oh, no!' she groaned. 'It's not going to work after all. We've forgotten about Mariella! We'll never get *her* to help.'

Sooze grinned, and flicked back a strand of bright lavender hair. 'Well, she doesn't have to know that's what she's doing, does she? You leave Mariella to me!'

'Twink, wake up! You've overslept!'

Bimi was shaking her by the shoulder. Blearily, Twink opened one eye – and then sat up with a start. Daffodil Branch was empty! Its moss beds

Bimi

were all neatly made up, without a fairy in sight.

'Where is everyone?' gasped Twink.

'They've already left for breakfast,' said Bimi. 'Hurry, you'll be late!'

'But where's Mrs Hover?' Twink threw back her daffodil-petal blanket and leapt out of bed, quickly smoothing her wings.

Bimi shook her head. 'I don't know. Oh, Twink, *hurry*!'

Her thoughts spinning, Twink flung on her

uniform. Why hadn't anyone woken her up? But there was no time to ask. Bimi was already racing for the door, half-flying in her hurry.

'Come on!' she called over her shoulder.

Wasps, they must really be late! Twink grabbed her oak-leaf cap and ran after her.

She reached the ledge outside the door and stopped short. Sunny was gone. Twink blinked. Sunny was *always* there, waiting patiently for her! What was going on?

Bimi had already taken off, skimming away towards the Great Branch in a blur of silver and gold.

'Wait!' Twink called after her. 'Sunny's gone! I can't – '

'Oh!' screamed Bimi suddenly. Stopping in midair, she clutched her left wing.

Twink rushed to the edge of the ledge. 'Bimi! What is it?'

'My wing! I've got a cramp!' Twink's heart iced over as Bimi began to fall. 'Help!' she shouted. She grew smaller and smaller as she plummeted towards the ground.

Without thinking, Twink launched herself off the ledge. Flapping her wings feverishly, she sped past classrooms and dorm branches, piercing through the air like an arrow. Bit by bit, the tumbling figure of Bimi grew closer as Twink gained on her.

They were nearing the ground now – oh, wasps, she wasn't going to make it! Twink put on an extra burst of speed, flying faster than she had ever thought possible.

'Hurry, Twink!' cried Bimi.

Her fingers brushed Bimi's . . . there! Twink grabbed Bimi's arm, her wings fluttering furiously to slow her down before they hit the ground. The two fairies landed in a heap on the soft moss carpet.

Phew! Twink sat up in a daze, breathing hard. 'Are you all right?' she asked.

'It worked!' shouted Bimi. Jumping up, she threw her arms around Twink. 'Twink, you flew! You really flew!'

Twink's mouth fell open as she realised. 'I – I did, didn't I?' she gasped.

Bimi's face was alight. She grabbed Twink's arms, jumping up and down. 'I knew you could do it!

Twink, you can fly!'

Suddenly all of Daffodil Branch was there, whooping and shouting, pounding her on the back. 'Twink, you did it! You really did it!'

Twink gasped as her friends caught her up in a jubilant hug.

'I can fly,' she whispered. She fluttered her wings and lifted up in the air, holding her breath. But nothing bad happened. Her wings didn't go berserk with fear. She was flying, just like any other fairy!

Twink did a sudden dip, dancing about over the others' heads. 'I can fly! I CAN FLY!'

And she was off, soaring up the great trunk of Glitterwings. Shrieking and laughing, Twink glided and dived, looping the loop and twirling in the air. She couldn't stop smiling. Her heart felt like it was shimmering with fairy dust.

Suddenly Sunny was there, flying around her with excited chirps. Twink flung her arms around his neck.

'Oh, Sunny!' she cried. 'I can fly!'

* * *

'We had it all planned,' laughed Pix at breakfast. 'It was Bimi's idea to pretend to have wing cramp, but you had to be all on your own, so that you'd have to fly! So we all got up really, really early this morning and snuck out of the Branch, taking Sunny with us –'

'He didn't argue at all!' broke in Sili, bouncing on her mushroom. 'I think he knew what we were up to.'

Twink's wings still tingled with the joy of flying. She could hardly wait to be up in the air again. 'How did you know I'd fly to save you?' she asked Bimi.

The blue-haired fairy smiled shyly. 'I remembered how you jumped to help Lola when she fell that time in Flight class. And I thought that maybe if someone else needed help, you wouldn't think about being scared – you'd just fly.'

Twink took another seed cake from the oak-leaf platter. 'Oh, Bimi, I'm so glad you were right!'

'Me too,' said Bimi with a sudden smile. 'I almost hit the ground for real!' Everyone laughed.

At the end of the table, Mariella's face was a thundercloud. Sooze nudged Twink and grinned. 'I told her we were playing a trick to get back at you for all those lines we had to do, so that you'd be late for breakfast and get into trouble. She could hardly wait to help us then!'

Mariella flushed and put down her acorn cup. 'Well, I don't know why everyone is making such a stupid fuss! It took you so long to fly that you'll probably never catch up with the rest of us anyway.'

'Especially Mariella,' squeaked Lola. 'She's a wonderful flyer.'

Twink rolled her eyes. Trust those two to try to dampen her spirits! But nothing could dampen them today. She smiled and rubbed her wings together, reliving the magic.

'But I still say *I* should have been the one to get to fall.' Sooze pretended to sulk, and then giggled and brushed her wing against Twink's. 'Opposite, isn't it glimmery? We can fly together to all our classes now!'

Twink hesitated, and glanced across at Bimi.

'Thanks, Sooze . . . but I'll be flying with Bimi,' she said softly.

'Oh!' Sooze looked taken aback, and was silent for a moment. 'Well . . . I suppose I'll carry on flying with Sili and Zena, then. But we're still Opposites, right?'

'Right!' said Twink. And it was true. Sooze was a wonderful friend when things were going well – but Twink knew now that she'd rather have a best friend who was wonderful *all* the time. She and Bimi smiled at each other.

A flutter of wings stirred the air as Mrs Lightwing landed beside their table. 'What's this I hear about a high-speed rescue this morning?' she said sternly, crossing her arms.

Twink jumped up, almost knocking over her cup of fresh morning dew. 'Mrs Lightwing! I can fly now, I can really fly!'

'So I've heard. It was hard to miss, the way you were shouting up and down the school! Is your wing better now, Bimi?' The Flight mistress gave Bimi a hard stare.

Bimi's pretty face reddened. 'I – I didn't really have wing cramp, Mrs Lightwing. We were just doing what you said – getting Twink in the air without her thinking about it.'

'And it worked!' cried Twink. 'Mrs Lightwing, it worked!'

'Yes, I see.' Mrs Lightwing tapped her wings together. 'But I'm not sure I approve of fairies pretending to fall all the way down the school!'

Daffodil Branch held its breath as Mrs Lightwing scanned the table. Then a small smile tugged at the corner of the Flight mistress's mouth, and suddenly Mrs Lightwing was beaming at them.

'Well done, Twink,' she said quietly, gripping Twink's shoulder. 'I knew you had it in you! I'm proud of you – of all of you,' she added, glancing at the others. 'It was a bit unorthodox, but you got her in the air!'

Twink glowed. 'Can I fly in the exhibition now?'

'The exhibition?' Mrs Lightwing looked startled. 'I'm afraid not. The other girls have been practising their routines for weeks now. You've only just started. You won't have the proper wing control.'

Twink felt herself colour up as Mariella smirked. 'But – but my parents will be here soon,' she stammered. 'I thought –'

Mrs Lightwing shook her head. 'Twink, I'm sorry. It really is too bad, but I just don't see how we could get you into good flying order by this afternoon. The answer is no.'

Chapter Seven

That morning the students polished every leaf of Glitterwings, and hung long streams of flowers from its branches. Pink and gold fairy dust shimmered in the air, spelling out the words *Welcome Friends and Families!*

The guests started arriving shortly before lunch. Twink waited on the front lawn with the other fairies from Daffodil Branch, scanning the sky for her parents.

'What am I going to tell them?' she asked Bimi. 'They'll expect me to be flying in the exhibition,

not doing a dance!'

'Just tell them the truth,' said Bimi sensibly. 'They'll be glad you can fly now, that's all.'

Twink sighed. She knew Bimi was right, but she still wished she could perform for her parents like everyone else.

Mariella and Lola landed on the grass nearby. 'Have you heard?' said Mariella loudly. 'They're going to give out prizes for the best fliers! What a shame there's not one for the best *dancer.*'

Twink's heart sank. She shrugged, trying to pretend she didn't mind.

'And *you're* sure to win the biggest prize of all, Mariella!' Lola fluttered her pale wings. 'You're the best there is!'

Mariella simpered, flipping back her silvery-green hair. 'Well, I didn't like to say so myself, but I do have a lot of natural talent.' She narrowed her eyes at Bimi. 'I just hope my *entire team* will fly their best too, so they don't let me down!'

'Don't worry,' snapped Bimi. 'But you know, Mariella, I think one of the Sixth Years is a lot likelier to win than you! They've got that amazing obstacle course they're flying through – it's a lot more impressive than a few barrel rolls from a First Year.'

Mariella scowled, but had no answer to this. She and Lola flitted off over the grass.

'Charming as ever!' said Twink.

Bimi shook her head. 'Oh, I don't mind Mariella so much. You know where you are with her – she's just nasty. But that little two-faced Lola! She's obviously forgotten all about how you saved her that time.'

Twink grinned. 'Well, I'm still glad that I didn't let her hit the ground, I suppose!'

Suddenly she recognised two familiar figures flying towards her, leading a mouse below them. She gave a squeal and shot up into the air. 'Look, my parents are here! And they've brought my little sister!'

All thoughts of wishing that her parents wouldn't come vanished as they landed, smiling broadly at her. Her father, tall and solid, with his familiar grin

and shock of dark purple hair. Her mother, calm and pretty, with her sudden laugh and bright pink locks. And Teena, trotting up on Brownie and practically jumping up and down in the stirrups, she was so excited!

Twink rushed into their arms. 'I'm so glad to see you!' she cried.

Her mother kissed her, and her father ruffled her hair. 'You're looking well!' he teased.

Teena gazed up at the giant oak in awe. 'Oh, it's wonderful!' she gasped.

Twink felt her chest swell with pride for her school. 'It is, isn't it?' she said. Then, remembering her manners, she quickly introduced Bimi to her parents, and knew from her mother's smile that she approved of her friend.

After that it seemed that all the other families arrived at once. Twink saw Sooze and her sister Winn talking happily with their parents. Mariella's mother had a pointed nose that stuck up in the air exactly like her daughter's. 'This isn't at all how it was done in *my* day!' Twink heard her say.

Bimi's mother was very beautiful, with elegant silver and gold wings and glistening blue hair, just like her daughter. She greeted Twink with a warm smile. 'I'm so glad Bimi's made a friend!' she said. 'I was worried that she might not. She's so shy, and she gets so prickly when she's nervous.'

Behind her, Twink saw Bimi scowling in embarrassment. 'Oh, we just ignore her when she's prickly,' she laughed. 'We know she doesn't really mean it!'

When all the families had arrived, the school butterflies streamed out of the tree, carrying woven-grass blankets and sweet seed cakes. A picnic! Twink and Bimi exchanged a delighted smile. In no time at all, the school was spread out on the mossy lawn, eating and drinking and laughing.

Between bites of seed cake, Twink chattered away to her parents, telling them all about the term so far. But somehow, she didn't mention the difficulties she'd had learning to fly. *I'll tell them soon,* she assured herself. *When the right moment comes.*

Finally a break came in the conversation. Twink

steeled her wings. 'Mum . . . Dad . . .' she started.

A group of sixth-year fairies swooped over the crowd like birds. 'The Flying Exhibition is about to begin!' they called through cupped hands. 'Students, get into your teams and see Mrs Lightwing for the flight order! Parents and families, please make your way to the flying field!'

Teena danced in place. 'Ooh, this is so exciting! Twink, what are you doing in the exhibition?'

Twink opened her mouth to speak, and then closed it again. 'I – I – oh, you'll see!' she managed weakly. 'Come on, Bimi, we'd better hurry.'

The two fairies flew towards the flying field. 'Why didn't you *tell* them?' demanded Bimi.

'I just couldn't.' Twink banked to avoid a slow-flying moth, and swallowed hard. 'Anyway, they'll find out soon enough.'

While the flying teams waited in oak-leaf tents, Twink stood alone at the side of the field, waiting for her cue to begin her dance. Looking around, she could see the hundreds of mushroom seats that had

Madame Brightfoot

been grown specially by Miss Petal for the exhibition – short ones in the front row and tall, thin ones in the back.

Madame Brightfoot flew over, her cobweb dress sparkling. 'Are you ready to dance, my child?' she cried.

Twink nodded. 'Yes, Madame.'

Madame Brightfoot clasped her hands together. 'Ah! It is the most beautiful dance I have made for you. Never mind that you are not in the air, everyone watching will be taken to the stars!'

Privately, Twink thought that the only stars today were going to be the flying teams! Never mind, she decided. If she had to do a dance, she'd do the best one in the world. She'd make her parents proud of her whether she was flying or not.

Finally, the mushroom grandstand was full. An expectant hush fell over the flying field. The bird and cricket orchestra began to play a lilting tune, and the first-year teams swooped out of the tent.

Now! Twink took a deep breath, and ran out to the middle of the field.

As the teams looped and twirled overhead, Twink concentrated on her steps. Turn, dip, sway, jump . . . Madame was right, she realised. It *was* a lovely dance! She forgot about not flying, and let the dance carry her away.

When the first-year teams flew back to the tent, Twink was almost sorry to see them go. Finishing her dance, she quickly tiptoed to the audience – and then stood stunned as a fresh wave of applause swept over her. They were applauding *her.* She must have done really well!

Excitement sparkled through Twink like fairy dust. Without thinking, she shot into the air and did three celebratory loop-the-loops, one after the other.

When she landed, the audience was laughing good-naturedly. Twink clapped a hand to her mouth. Oh, wasps! What would Mrs Lightwing say now? Her face on fire, she raced off the field just as the second-year team flew on.

After the exhibition, the students mingled with their families and friends on the flying lawn, sipping sweet nectar served by the butterflies. The Sixth Years were allowed to wear their own clothes for the occasion, and looked very grown-up in their sparkly shorts and tops.

'Twink, that was wonderful. We're so proud of you!' Twink's mother enveloped her in a hug.

'Even though I didn't fly?' Twink thought she knew the answer, but she still wanted to hear her mother say it.

Her mother laughed, fluttering her lavender wings. 'But, Twink, you *did* fly. You did three

118

perfect loop-the-loops!'

'We're very proud of you, Twinkster,' said her father gently. 'You got the hang of it in the end. We knew you would.'

Twink's mouth dropped open. 'You – you *knew* I couldn't fly? But –'

'Miss Shimmery wrote to us weeks ago,' said Twink's mother. 'We all decided that the best thing was for you to come to it in your own time – and you did.'

'But we wanted to be here for you today, either way,' added her father. He squeezed her shoulder. 'To congratulate or commiserate!'

Madame Brightfoot landed beside them. 'What do you think of this wonderful dancer girl?' she cried. Twink's parents turned away to speak to her, and Twink and Bimi looked at each other in amazement.

'They never said a word!' said Twink in an undertone.

'I suppose they trusted you to work it out on your own,' said Bimi. 'That was pretty glimmery of them.'

'And of the school, really,' said Twink thought-fully. 'They did everything they could to help me not be so afraid, but in the end it was down to me – well, with a bit of help from my friends!' She and Bimi grinned at each other.

Teena's eyes were wide, going from one to the other. 'What?' she demanded. 'What are you talking about?'

Twink scooped her little sister into a hug. 'I'll tell you someday when you're older!' she promised. She took off her oak-leaf cap and popped it on to Teena's bright pink hair. 'Look, you're a Glitterwings girl already!'

When it was time for the flying prizes to be announced, everyone gathered around the mossy platform where Miss Shimmery and the teachers waited.

The HeadFairy hovered above the crowd, her rainbow wings glinting in the sun. 'With so many talented fliers here today, it hasn't been easy to decide on the winners, but Mrs Lightwing and I have done our best!'

Mariella, standing nearby, smirked. 'I'm sure they'll choose me,' Twink heard her say to her mother. 'No one in our year can hold a glow-worm to me.'

'We'll start with our First Years,' said Miss Shimmery from the platform. 'It was a very difficult choice, but the best flier in the first year is . . . Sooze Birdsong!'

The entire first year burst into wild applause. Sooze screeched with delight, and flitted to the stage to collect her prize.

'Oh!' Mariella's wings snapped shut.

'How outrageous!' huffed her mother. 'You're far more talented, Mariella!'

Twink watched Sooze collect a scroll and a kiss from Miss Shimmery, and smiled. *Well done, Opposite,* she thought. Even though they weren't best friends any more, she was still pleased for Sooze. All that practising she had done had paid off!

After Miss Shimmery had announced the best fliers from all the years, she held up her hands for silence. 'Now then. There's still one more prize to

give . . . that of the best flier in the entire school.'

Mariella and her mother perked up, their eyes gleaming.

'Oh, no,' Twink murmured to Bimi. 'There may be hope for Mariella yet!'

Miss Shimmery smiled at the crowd. 'Mrs Lightwing suggested to me who deserves this prize the most, and I wholeheartedly agree with her. It's unusual to give this prize for only three loop-the-loops . . . but I think you'll understand when I explain that the fairy in question only learned how to fly this morning.'

Twink's heart skipped a beat. Miss Shimmery looked directly at her.

'Twink Flutterby, please fly forward and collect your prize!'

'Oh, Twink!' gasped Bimi, clutching her arm. 'You've won!'

Twink stood without moving, certain that she had heard wrong. Her father laughed and pushed her gently between the wings. 'Go on, Twinkster – everyone's waiting for you!'

In a dream, Twink flew to the stage. Everyone was cheering. Miss Shimmery handed her a scroll and a small golden brooch embossed with the Glitterwings Academy emblem – an oak tree with wings.

'Well done, Twink.' She kissed Twink's cheek. 'I'm so glad – we knew you could do it.'

Mrs Lightwing gave her a hug. 'Those were some very impressive loops for a new flier, my girl!'

'Thank you!' gasped Twink, clutching her prizes. 'Oh, thank you!'

As the day ended, the Daffodil Branch fairies gathered on the front lawn, saying quick goodbyes before flying home with their families for the holiday.

'Hurrah for Sooze and Twink!' cried Pix, punching the air. 'We've got *both* the first year prizewinners in Daffodil Branch – how glimmery is that?'

'Yes, aren't we wonderful?' laughed Sooze, flying up and doing a somersault in the air.

Mariella scowled. 'Well, *I* don't think it's so wonderful,' she snapped. 'The contest was obviously unfair!'

Lola linked arms with her. 'Never mind, Mariella,' she sniffed. 'You didn't want their silly prizes anyway!'

'Oh, yes she did,' laughed Sooze, dangling her scroll in front of Mariella. 'Never mind, better luck next time!'

Mariella batted Sooze's scroll away from her face with a glare. She and Lola skimmed quickly away over the grass, whispering behind their hands.

Poor Mariella! thought Twink. She had brought

this on herself, but now she'd never live it down. Twink's new brooch was pinned to her uniform, winking in the last rays of sunlight. She touched it gently, still hardly able to believe what had happened.

'You deserve it!' said Bimi, watching her. 'You really do, Twink.'

Twink smiled gratefully at her. 'Thanks, but they should have given you a prize, as well. I couldn't have done it without your help.'

Bimi nudged Twink with her wing. 'That's what friends are for. I'm just glad you didn't let me fall!'

Sooze threw her arms around Twink's and Bimi's shoulders, her wings fluttering madly. 'We should have a party to celebrate when we get back – a midnight feast!'

Twink laughed. Sooze would never change! 'That sounds great! What do you think, Bimi?' She grinned at her best friend.

Bimi nodded enthusiastically, her blue hair gleaming. 'Definitely. We'll get rid of Mrs Hover somehow and celebrate!'

'Think again, girls,' said a stern voice.

Mrs Hover! The fairies winced as the plump matron appeared in their midst, flapping her wings grimly. 'There'll be no midnight feasts when you get back, or any other time!'

'Oh, we didn't mean it really, Hovey!' said Sooze. She winked at the other fairies behind Mrs Hover's back.

'Twink!' called Twink's mother with a smile. 'Come on now, it's time to leave.'

After a last hug for her friends, Twink skimmed off into the twilight. As she and her family started off on the journey home, she glanced over her shoulder at Glitterwings. The flowers for the exhibition were still draped over its branches, swaying in the breeze. Tiny golden windows spiralled up the great trunk.

Twink's heart swelled. Oh, it had been a perfect day, the best day ever! She had learned how to fly, she had made a new best friend . . . and she went to the most wonderful school in the world.

To find out about other glimmery Glitterwings Academy stories, turn over the page

Titania Woods

There are lots more stories about Glitterwings
Academy – make sure you haven't missed any of them!

	Midnight Feast	978 0 7475 9209 9
	Friends Forever	978 0 7475 9208 2
	Fairy Dust	978 0 7475 9207 5
	Fledge Star	978 0 7475 9206 8
	Term-Time Trouble	978 0 7475 9205 1
	New Girl	978 0 7475 9204 4
	Seedling Exams	978 0 7475 9203 7
	Christmas Fairy	978 0 7475 9835 0
	Sister Secrets	978 0 7475 9831 2
	Treasure Hunt	978 0 7475 9832 9
	Friendship Dance	978 0 7475 9833 6
	Magical Mayhem	978 0 7475 9834 3

If you have any difficulty in finding these in your local bookshop,
please visit www.bloomsbury.com or call 020 7440 2475
to order direct from Bloomsbury Publishing.

Visit www.glitterwingsacademy.co.uk for more fabulous fairy fun!